MOIN

AND THE

MONSTER

Read more by Anushka Ravishankar from Duckbill
Moin the Monster Songster

Other books by Anushka Ravishankar
Tiger on a Tree
Catch That Crocodile
Elephants Never Forget
One Two Tree!
Today Is My Day
Excuse Me, Is This India?
Wish You Were Here
To Market! To Market!
The Fivetongued Firefanged Folkadotted Dragon Snake
Alphabets Are Amazing Animals
Anything but a Grabooberry
I Like Cats
Excuses! Excuses!
Song of the Bookworm
Where's the Baby Gone?
The Rumour
The Boy Who Drew Cats
The Monkeys and the Capseller
The Shepherd Boy
The Goose That Laid Golden Eggs
The Fox and the Crow
The Hare and the Tortoise
The Storyteller: Tales from the Arabian Nights
Zain and Ana: At Least a Fish
Zain and Ana: Ghosts Don't Eat
Zain and Ana: Just Like a Bug
Puppets Unlimited with Everyday Materials
Toys and Tales with Everyday Materials
Masks and Performance with Everyday Materials
Trash! On Ragpicker Children and Recycling

MOIN

AND THE

MONSTER

Anushka Ravishankar

Illustrations by
Anitha Balachandran

duckbill

Duckbill Books

Venkat Towers, 165, P.H. Road, Maduravoyal
Chennai 600 095
www.duckbill.in
platypus@duckbill.in

Published by Duckbill Books and westland ltd

10 9 8 7 6 5 4 3 2 1

ISBN: 978-93-81626-90-0

Typeset by Ram Das Lal
Cover by Anitha Balachandran

Printed at Thomson Press (India) Ltd.

Also available as an ebook

Children's reading levels vary widely. The general reading
levels are indicated by colour on the back cover. There are
three levels: younger readers, middle readers and young
adult readers. Within each level, the position of the dot
indicates the reading complexity. Books for young
adults may contain some slightly mature material.

MOIN GETS A MONSTER

MONSTER RULE I

Every monster has to obey the monster rules without asking any awkward questions.

One night, in the dim darkness of his room, Moin heard something shuffling and sniffling under his bed.

'Who's that?' he squeaked.

'A bonster,' said a shrieky kind of voice.

Moin flashed his torchlight all over the room. Nothing.

'Abonster, where are you?' he asked in a wobbly whisper.

'A MONSTER, stupid, not a bonster.'

'A m-m-monster? Where are you?' asked Moin.

'Udder the bed, obviously. Widd a very dusty old suitcase add a pair of blue socks which are horrible and sbelly. That's why I'b holding by dose.'

'Oh! So that's where they are. I was looking for those socks.'

The pair of rolled-up blue socks came shooting out from under the bed and hit Moin on the nose as he leaned out of bed.

'OW! Thanks. But … but why are you under the bed?'

'How do I know? That's where monsters always are. Some stupid monster rule, I suppose. If I knew all the rules I wouldn't be here.'

MONSTER RULE 42

When a monster is sent to the human world, it has to hide under the bed. If there is no bed, it can hide under a cupboard or any other suitable piece of furniture. If there is no suitable piece of furniture, it should look for a dark corner.

Moin flashed the light under the bed. 'But I can't see you.'

'That's another monster rule. You can only see me if you draw me.'

Moin was confused. 'But I can only draw you if I see you,' he said.

'If you don't draw me, I'll have to stay invisible forever.'

Moin didn't reply. He had a feeling that an invisible monster was better than a visible one.

'You have to draw me!' the monster shouted. 'It's the monster rule!'

'But I'm not a monster,' Moin pointed out.

'If you disobey the rule you'll … you'll … you'll turn into a … a … suitcase!'

'But how can I draw you when I don't know how you look?'

'I can describe myself, can't I? Then you can draw me.'

Moin was not at all sure about this. Once, in art class, he had drawn a horse and the teacher had thought it was a map of Maharashtra. So now, he labelled all his drawings carefully. And even then his art teacher always wrote 'Ha!' on his paper.

Still, he didn't feel like turning into a suitcase. Suitcases were rectangular and boring and people were always sitting on them or pushing them under beds. So he switched on the light, got out his crayons and a piece of paper and waited for the monster to describe itself.

'You can't draw me on that tiny bit of paper!' the monster told him. 'I'll be as big as you draw me, and I don't want to be the size of your foot.'

'But I don't have any bigger sheets of paper.'

'What do you mean, you don't have any bigger sheets! You have to get a bigger sheet! You have to! You have to! YOU HAVE TO!'

'Okay! Okay!' said Moin. 'I have an idea.'

He took the calendar off the wall, selected a month that had passed, tore off the sheet and turned it around. 'There. That's the biggest sheet I can get, and if you don't like it, there's nothing I can do about it. So describe yourself.'

'Humph,' said the monster, and began to sing in a high pitch which sounded quite horrible with its shrieky voice:

Eyes like flames
And nose like pails
Ears like horns
And teeth like nails
A scary, fearsome sight to see
Monster, monster, monster me!

'Wait a minute!' shouted Moin. 'What do you mean, nose like pails? You mean you have more than one nose?'

'Oh baah, what a silly boy I've got. I mean my nostrils are as deep as buckets, of course.'

'Why can't you say what you mean, then?'

'It's obvious to all but the meanest intelligence.'

'What?'

'That's a clever way of saying you're stupid.'

'Some people are so stupid, they can't even say what they mean,' muttered Moin.

The monster started singing again:

Skull-shaped mole
On rock-like chin
Long green hair
And purple skin
In the dark you'll scream to see
Monster, monster, monster ME!

Drum-shaped chest
And arms like trees
Bamboo legs on
Feet like skis
Terrifying as can be
Monster, monster, monster MEEEEEEEEEE!

There was silence, as Moin drew the monster, part by part, slowly, carefully and precisely.

'Have you finished?' asked the monster.

'Shhhh … can't you see I'm drawing?'

'Finished?' asked the monster after half a minute.

'Wait!' said Moin, erasing a rather large ear.

The monster waited for half a minute more. 'Finished?'

'Almost,' said Moin. 'Right, here you are.'

'Now hold up the paper,' the monster said.

'I'll look at it as if I'm looking into a mirror. Then I'll appear.'

So Moin held up the paper.

And ...

'EEEEEK!' said the monster.

'Eeeeeeek!' said Moin, startled to see his drawing suddenly turn into a live creature.

'Owowowowow! What have you done? What have you done?' wailed the monster.

'Why? What's the matter?'

'This is not how I should look,' wept the monster. 'I'm *fearsome*. You've made me look funny!'

'I've drawn you *exactly* as you described yourself,' said Moin, miffed. He thought he'd done a splendid job of drawing the monster. 'I can't help it if you don't know how to describe yourself.'

'I'm supposed to be purple.'

'Oh, yes, um … sorry. I ran out of purple so I used the closest colour I could find.'

'Pink? Bright pink is closest to purple? And why are my legs so *thin*?'

'They're bamboos, aren't they? That's what you said—bamboo legs.'

'These are not bamboos, they're drumsticks. If I don't watch where I'm going, some cook will pluck them off and make a sambar of them.'

'What rubbish! Drumsticks don't look like that.'

'Bamboos don't look like this either. And what are these *things* I have instead of feet?'

'Skis, of course.'

'These? You call these skis? They look like blue brooms.'

'I don't know what skis look like. I guessed. I'm very good at guessing. They look kind of ski-ish to me. You know, skittish and blue and kind of brushy.'

'And which animal has horns like these?'

'Oh, were they supposed to be animal horns? I thought you meant the kind of horns that autorickshaws have.'

'You mean I'm going to be walking around with *autorickshaw* horns? Oh, woe!'

'You complain too much,' said Moin.

'Of course I'll complain, look at this—you've drawn my teeth upside down! How am I going to eat with these blunt nail-heads?'

'If you wanted them with the sharp side down you should have said so. I can't read your stupid mind, can I?'

'So many millions of children in the world, and I had to get the one child who can't draw,' sobbed the monster.

'Then go find some other stupid child,' said Moin, throwing down his crayons. 'I didn't ask you to crawl under the bed and wake me up and make me draw all kinds of things in the middle of the night. Go away and find some great painter. Go and hide under Picasso's bed.'

'I can't. Now that you've drawn me, I have to stay with you. Besides, Picasso's dead.'

'Forever?' asked Moin, alarmed.

'Once people die, they're usually dead forever.'

'No, I mean are you going to stay with me forever?'

'Forever,' nodded the monster glumly. 'That's the rule.'

'Oh no,' said Moin.

'Exactly,' said the monster.

MONSTER RULE 54

A monster has to stay forever with the human who has given it a body. (Also see rules number 71, 228 and 364.)

GOING BANANAS

Moin sat in waiting room of the doctor's clinic. He was not sick, but his mother would not believe it.

On Friday, Moin's father, Mr Kaif, had bought a huge bunch of bananas home. This had caused a bit of a fuss.

'What are we going to do with so many bananas?' Moin's mother wanted to know.

'Eat them?' his father suggested.

'You know bananas make me burp. You know Moin's not terribly fond of bananas either. So why on earth did you buy so many bananas?'

Mr Kaif looked sheepish. Mrs Kaif guessed immediately. It was not the first time this had happened. Whenever he saw a poor man trying to sell something, Mr Kaif felt so sorry for him that he bought up everything the man was selling. He had once come home with forty-three straw baskets of various sizes. They had had to gift straw baskets at every birthday and anniversary for months after that. Their own house was full of straw baskets in various avatars.

But this time things were more difficult. There were no birthdays in the next couple of days, and anyway, it wasn't likely that anybody would want bananas as their birthday gift.

That night, Mrs Kaif made banana fritters for dinner and Mr Kaif made a pudding with bananas and coconut and jaggery. Then they

had a banana each as an after-dinner snack. At the end of it, Mrs Kaif burped fifty-seven times without stopping and Moin declared that he would never eat another banana in his life.

So Mrs Kaif was astonished to see him go to his room with a big bunch of bananas the next morning.

MONSTER RULE 7

A monster can eat anything it wants.

'That boy is unpredictable,' she told her husband, who was desperately searching the internet for more banana-based recipes.

Mr Kaif grunted. He had just found the recipe for a banana burger, which sounded quite awful, but would use up as many as eight bananas.

Throughout the day Moin kept going to his room with bunches of bananas, and coming out with piles of banana peels. Even Mr Kaif started getting a bit alarmed.

'Do you think he's flushing them down the toilet?' he asked.

The next time Moin went in with a bunch of bananas, Mr and Mrs Kaif pressed their ears to Moin's bathroom wall.

'What are you two doing?' Moin asked curiously, as he passed by behind them, carrying another pile of peels.

'What have you been doing with those bananas?'

'Eating them, of course,' Moin said, batting his long eyelashes and trying to look innocent.

'Oh dear,' said Moin's mother and immediately called up the doctor.

'But I'm not sick,' Moin protested.

'You will be, soon. Prevention is better than cure.'

Nothing Moin said could change Mrs Kaif's mind. So there he was, at the doctor's clinic, waiting for his turn.

'It's all your fault!' Moin whispered to his pocket. The monster had hopped into it just as he was leaving. It had flattened itself till it was as thin as a piece of paper, folded itself up and slipped in.

MONSTER RULE 64

While travelling in the human world, a monster can flatten and fold itself to fit into a small space.

'What do you mean, my fault. I have to eat, don't I? Do you want me to starve?'

'Starve? You were shovelling bananas into your mouth like a hippopotamus in a circus,' said Moin. 'Starve!'

A small girl sitting across from Moin was staring at him fixedly, her chin in her hands.

She had a steady stream of snot trickling down her nose and dripping on to the floor. Her mother was reading a magazine. From time to time, the girl wiped her nose on her mother's sari.

'Look Mummy,' she said suddenly. 'That boy is talking to his pocket. And his pocket is jumping.'

Moin gave her a nasty look and held his pocket down hard. Mrs Kaif got up, scooped him up and swept into the doctor's office. An old man who was before them in the queue squawked angrily, 'I'm next! I'm next!' but Mrs Kaif ignored him.

'Doctor! I think my son is having a heart attack!' she screamed. 'Look, he's clutching his chest. It's all because of the bananas!'

She was in such a state of panic that the doctor had to give her some medicine to calm her down. Moin, meanwhile, was muttering to his pocket.

'Can't you keep still for a few seconds? Stop fluttering around like that! You'll get me into even more trouble.'

Fortunately, the doctor and Mrs Kaif were too busy calming and being calmed to pay attention to Moin. When Mrs Kaif had got over her panic, she explained the situation to the doctor.

'And he doesn't even like bananas!' she said finally.

The doctor told Moin's mother to deworm him.

'But what about his heart? He was clutching it!'

'I was just scratching my chest,' Moin said quickly.

'Are you sure bananas don't cause heart attacks?'

'Don't worry,' said the doctor in his smooth, calm-the-stupid–patient-down–and–charge-her-a-fat-bill voice. 'He just needs to be dewormed. Maybe the worms in his stomach like bananas. Hee, hee! Hee, hee, hee!'

Neither Moin nor his mother laughed at the joke. The doctor ruffled Moin's hair. Moin glared at him, and wished the doctor had hair so that he could ruffle it right back. But unfortunately, the doctor was bald as an egg.

So he blew a spit bubble instead, and the doctor quickly let him go.

'It's not his heart, it's his head that needs examining,' he muttered. Luckily for him, Mrs Kaif didn't hear him.

'The worm's not in my stomach, it's in my pocket,' muttered Moin. Luckily, Mrs Kaif didn't hear that either.

That night, dinner was banana burgers, followed by a sticky banana halwa. Moin didn't dare tell anyone how sick he felt at the very thought of bananas. He was afraid that would cause another dash to the egg-bald doctor.

And when he went to his room the sight he saw made his stomach churn like a banana milkshake. The monster was lolling on Moin's bed, eating the bananas Moin had smuggled in just before dinner. The banana peels were lying in a heap on the floor, and when Moin entered, the monster was trying to eat one of them

'Ugh,' said the monster, 'I wonder why the skin doesn't taste as good as the insides?'

Moin felt too queasy to reply.

'You know, it's a good thing we discovered that I like bananas. I've never eaten them before, but they seem just the right food for me. Yum.'

That was when Moin got the idea. Since it was the monster who was eating all the bananas, it was obviously the monster who ought to be dewormed. He went and asked his mother for the deworming medicine.

'Here it is,' said Mrs Kaif, burping in approval. 'It's nice to see how responsible he's becoming,' she burped to Mr Kaif. 'He's actually asking for his medicine.'

But Mr Kaif was busy copying down a recipe for banana pulao and didn't hear a word she said.

Moin went into his room, with the bottle in his pocket. The monster was making a design on the floor with the banana skins. The whole room smelt of bananas. Moin's stomach did a quick somersault. He held his breath and began to collect the peels.

'Hey! You're ruining my work of art!' yelled the monster.

'Agmblph,' said Moin, and rushed out of the room with the peels.

When he came back the monster was sulking on the windowsill.

'Look what I've got for you!' Moin told it.

'Bananas?' asked the monster, and scowled when it saw the bottle that Moin was holding up.

'It's a special drink,' Moin said.

'I don't want it.'

'It's very, very yummy,' he chanted. Which wasn't quite true.

'No.'

'It's limey-limey-lemony,' he sang. It wasn't really a lie, because the bottle did say 'in a lemon-flavoured base'.

'So?'

'It's fizzy-wizzy-dizzy!' he yodelled. This was a lie.

'Huh.'

It's a yummy-wummy, lime-n-lemony,
Fizzy-wizzy drink!
It gives you strength and energy,
It gives you brains to think.

These were lies too.

'STOP!' yelled the monster. 'Please stop!'

Moin stopped. 'Drink it,' he said, 'I'm going to keep singing till you drink it.'

'It's yummy-wummy,' he began again.

The monster grabbed the bottle from Moin, and drank up the deworming medicine.

MONSTER RULE 112

Food fit for humans is not always fit for monsters.

'Yaaargh! Btooooie! Glbrghch!' it yelled. It held its throat and began to spin round and round so fast that it looked like a fuzzy ball of pink.

Then it fell on the floor and began to roll around the room. Faster and faster it rolled, till it hit the wall on one end, then it rolled the other way, till it hit the wall again. Finally, it stopped and got up shakily. While Moin watched in horror, wondering what would happen next, the monster began to sing:

Blechity blachety, tootem and goo
The gerbin is blicking
The quamit is poo.

Suddenly there was a loud banging on the door.

'Stop, monster, stop!' whispered Moin.

The monster didn't stop.

Twickety twackety dillick and doo
The flimball is chicking
The vimbag is too.

Moin picked up the monster, pushed it into the cupboard where all the bedsheets and things were kept, and opened the door.

'What is going on here?' asked Moin's mother.

'Yes, what's going on?' asked his father. 'We heard a strange kind of wailing.'

'It was me, I was singing,' said Moin. 'Listen.'

And he started to sing in a high pitch, which he hoped would sound like the monster's horrible voice:

Twickety twackety hollow herring
I sing what I like
So I like what I sing.

'STOP!' shouted Moin's mother.

'Hmm,' said Moin's father, at a loss for words.

'Shall I sing the next bit for you?' asked Moin.

'NO!' shouted Moin's mother.

'Come, come,' said Mr Kaif, finding words again, 'If he's so keen on singing, we must encourage him. No need to sing now,' he said quickly, when Moin opened his mouth to continue, 'but tomorrow, Moin, you will join a singing class.'

Moin stared at him in horror, and couldn't say a word.

'Make sure it's far away from here,' he heard his mother whisper, as they went away. 'Otherwise the neighbours will complain.'

Moin closed the door and opened the cupboard. The monster looked at him with a happy smile and a loud hiccup. Moin scowled back.

'Singing classes! Now look what you've done.'

'Have a banana,' said the monster and fell asleep on the pile of bedsheets.

Moin went to sleep and dreamed he was singing on stage, while the audience threw squishy bananas at him, and Mr and Mrs Kaif sat in the audience, smiling proudly.

Return Gift

Moin was singing a new raag with his singing teacher. He was scowling. He didn't dislike singing, and he even liked his teacher, Tothogotho Chowdhury; it was difficult to dislike someone with a name like Tothogotho.

Chowdhuryji had, for some reason, taken a great liking to Moin. He smiled gummily at him, shook his shabby, long, grey hair, and said 'Bhalo!' every time Moin sang a note.

Today, the music teacher was more pleased than usual. Moin was singing with all his might, and Chowdhuryji thought the boy was inspired. So he kept making the raag more and more difficult.

Actually, Moin was just angry. He had to go to a birthday party, but he was going to be late because of the singing class. His father

wouldn't let him miss it. The angrier Moin
got, the better he sang. The better Moin sang,
the more his teacher taught him. So, by the
time Moin had finished his class, it was very
late, and he had to run all the way home. He
reached panting and sweating and in a very
bad mood.

'What are you giving Parvati?' his mother
asked him, as she opened the door.

Moin had completely forgotten about the
birthday gift.

Mrs Kaif dug out another one of the straw
baskets, but she suddenly remembered that
they had given a straw basket to Parvati's

parents on their wedding anniversary. She felt that it might be a bit odd to give a straw basket again on Parvati's birthday.

Moin didn't want to stop off to buy a gift, because he was already late. So he looked through his desk hoping to find something he could give. There was a nice shiny green pen, but he had chewed its end flat. There was a book about the planets, which he'd never read and which still looked quite new. But when he opened it Moin saw that it said, 'To Moin, Happy Birthday, from Parvati.' So that was out. Moin opened his cupboard.

'I'm bored,' said the monster as soon as it saw Moin. It had taken to lolling around on the pile of sheets all day long.

The most wicked, brilliant idea flashed through Moin's head.

'Would you like to come for a party?' he asked the monster.

'Yes!' the monster leaped up. 'Will I get bananas?'

'I don't know, but there'll be lots of other delicious food,' said Moin. 'And lots of singing and dancing and games. But there's one problem—I have to wrap you up.'

The monster looked suspicious.

'Anyone who's not invited but wants to go to the party has to dress up as a birthday gift,' said Moin. 'It's one of the Birthday Rules. You know what rules are like; you can't understand them, you just have to obey them.'

The monster nodded. It knew all about rules. The Monster Rules were a part of every monster's primary education. So it flattened itself to a nice wrappable shape, and Moin packed it up in bright wrapping paper.

MONSTER RULE I

Every monster has to obey the monster rules without asking any awkward questions.

'And remember, no moving and *definitely* no singing.'

'So what are you giving Parvati?' Mrs Kaif asked Moin as she zipped to Parvati's house on her scooter, with Moin at the back.

'Er ... it's a drawing I drew,' said Moin, trying desperately not to fall off the scooter. He had the monster in one hand, and with the other hand he held on tight to the metal rod behind his seat.

'That's lovely. It's so much nicer to give something you've made yourself. It shows that you really care about the person. She'll be so happy,' said Mrs Kaif.

'A drawing?' asked Parvati, disgusted, when Moin gave her the gift. 'Who wants a drawing

that you drew? You draw horribly.' She
chucked the packet on a pile of gifts.

'Ow!' yelled the monster.

'Shut up,' hissed Moin, and went off to join
the rest of the children. They were just about
to cut the cake.

Happy birthday to you!
Happy birthday to you
Happy birthday dear Parvati
Happy birthday to you!!!

they sang.

Suddenly Moin noticed a familiar gruff, high-
pitched voice singing along. Though it sang the
same tune, the words were completely different.

The children sang:

From good friends and true
From old friends and new
Happy birthday dear Parvati
Happy birthday tooooo yooooooou!

But the voice sang:

Gummy halwa to cheeeew
And cakes dripping goooo

Soggy sandwiches, oily samosas
And sharbat like gluuuueee.

Moin looked around. The monster had torn
its way out of the packet and was standing on
the pile of gifts, singing at the top of its shrieky
voice. Moin raced towards it, and was just
about to clamp its mouth shut with his palm,
when the children stopped singing.

In the silence, only the monster's horrible
voice could be heard:

'Uuuuuuuuuuuuuue!' it went.

Everyone turned to look. Moin froze. The
monster stopped singing, and smirked.

'That was brilliant, Moin!' said Mrs
Moorthy, Parvati's mother. 'I didn't know
you'd learnt ventriloquism.'

'Er yes,' said Moin. He had no idea what
she was talking about.

'And is that your dummy? So creative!'

'It's a dummy alright,' Moin muttered,
trying to hold the monster still.

'Oh my goodness,' Mrs Moorthy said to
Parvati, 'who would have thought our Moin was
so talented? Look how he's made his dummy
with recycled material! Autorickshaw horns, old
brooms, branches. Quite marvellous!'

Then she turned to the children and said,
'Children, we were planning to play Passing

the Parcel, but since Moin as brought his wonderful dummy along, why don't we have a ventriloquism show by Moin instead? Let's eat, then we'll have a little show by our little ventriloquist and his lovely dummy.'

Moin nearly fainted with shock. For one thing, she had called the monster lovely. Besides, he had no idea what she was talking about. He hissed to his friend Tony, 'What's a ventri-whatever-she-said?'

Tony was as good as an encyclopaedia. There were very few things he didn't know, and this could be quite irritating for his friends who knew very few things. But he was useful to have around.

'Ventriloquism is when you throw your voice so that it seems to be coming from somewhere else. That's what you did just now. You sang, and it looked as if your dummy was singing.'

Moin decided to let that pass. This was not the time or place to inform Tony how mistaken he was.

Soon after everyone had finished eating, Mrs Moorthy dragged an unwilling Moin and made all the children sit before him in rows. She gave him a chair and a small table for the dummy. Moin had been feeding the monster bits of cake and samosa to keep it quiet, so now it was looking a bit sleepy, but happy. Moin was not at all sure it would say or do anything.

'Er, what do you want it to say?'

'That's for you to decide, Moin,' Mrs Moorthy said. 'Whatever you like. Right, children?'

The children, who would have much preferred to play Passing the Parcel, scowled at Moin. Moin sighed. He had no idea what to do.

'Can I ask it a question?' Tony called out.

'Okay.'

'What's your name?'

The monster did not reply. Moin shook it. 'Tell them your name,' he hissed.

'Don't have one,' the monster said drowsily.

The children sniggered.

'Sing a song then,' Parvati said. She was hoping Moin would hurry up and finish, so that she could get on with her party.

The monster immediately came wide awake, stood up on the table and began to sing:

Sing, sing, sing
Sing a little song
Ping, ping, ping
Ping a little pong

King, king, king
King a little kong

Wring, wring, wring
Wring a little wrong

Bring, bring, bring
Bring a little brong
Fling, fling, fling
Fling a little flong

Ting, ting, ting—

Moin had a terrible time of it. When the monster sang, it wanted to dance. So Moin had to pretend that he was moving the monster's hands and legs. By the end of the third stanza, he was panting and his arms were aching from trying to catch hold of the monster's arms and legs at the same time, but his audience was loving it. They were rolling on the floor laughing, and those who were not were trying to imitate the monster's strange dance.

Finally, Moin grabbed the monster and ran off to Parvati's room, yelling, 'Have to go to the loo!' because the monster showed no signs of stopping.

Half the children ran after him saying, 'Give us the dummy!'

But Moin ran into the room and banged the door shut on their surprised faces.

After a few minutes, Parvati knocked at the door.

'Moin, finished?'

'Have they all gone?' Moin hissed.

'There's only us!' Tony called out.

Moin opened the door and let Parvati and Tony in.

When they entered, they saw the monster trying to do a headstand on Parvati's bed.

'Wh-wh-what?'

'Wh-who?'

'It's not a dummy, it's a real monster,' Moin told them.

'But, but, but,' said Parvati, unable to get over the sight of the monster who was now trying to burrow under her pillow.

Suddenly there was a knock at the door.

'Time for Passing the Parcel!' Mrs Moorthy called out brightly.

'Coming, Amma!' Parvati called out. 'We'll have to go! What should we do?'

Tony was watching the monster, fascinated. 'A monster! A real monster! It doesn't look like anything I imagined.'

The monster stood up. 'Exactly! This is what I've been trying to tell him. Monsters are ferocious, not—'

'We'll talk about that later,' Moin said quickly. 'Let's leave it some food, and lock the door.'

So while the children played Passing the Parcel and Tailing the Donkey, the monster ate fifteen samosas, five slices of cake, eleven barfis and a whole large packet of chips.

After all the others had left, Parvati, Tony and Moin went back to the room. The monster was snoring in Parvati's bed, his head under her pillow. Moin told them the whole story.

'So,' he finished, 'now it's all yours, Parvati. Happy birthday!'

'You can keep it,' said Parvati. 'It eats too much. And I don't like its singing, it gives me a headache.'

'I wouldn't mind keeping it,' said Tony, 'But you know I share the room with my grandfather. If I ask him to share it with a monster, he may not like it.'

'And anyway,' said the monster drowsily from under Parvati's pillow, 'it's against monster rules. You can't give me away.'

MONSTER RULE 114

A monster cannot be gifted away.

'What's that?' asked Mrs Kaif. 'Didn't you give Parvati her present?'

'Oh this!' said Moin. 'This is a return gift.'

MONSTER AT SCHOOL

'I want to go to school,' said the monster.

'Too bad, they don't admit monsters into my school,' Moin said.

'I don't want to join your stupid school. I just want to go with you. I'm bored. Besides, it's been a long time since I met Tony. I've remembered a few more rules. I should tell them to Tony before I forget.'

Tony and the monster had hit it off very well. Whenever Tony tried to tell his friends interesting facts, they said things like, 'Hey encyclopaedia, please go and tell someone else.' But the monster liked listening to Tony. And Tony was very interested in learning about the monster world. He was trying to make up a list of the monster rules. The monster could remember only a few of them, and not in order. But Tony was writing them down, leaving gaps for the ones that the monster couldn't remember. So far he had about eight rules and one hundred and three gaps.

'I don't know why Tony bothers. Bet you've made up half the rules.'

'We're not allowed to make up rules,' the monster said haughtily, as they set off for school, with the monster in Moin's pocket.

MONSTER RULE 18

A monster cannot make up rules.

'Ha,' said Moin, because he could think of nothing else to say. He thought hard for something really insulting to call the monster, because he was irritated at it for going with him to school. 'Mary's little lamb,' he said, finally.

'If I'm the lamb, you're Mary,' said the monster, from Moin's pocket.

Moin had nothing to say to that. So he sulked all the way to school.

The day began badly. As soon as the prayer song started at the morning assembly, Moin's pocket started to dance and sing in a shrieky voice.

The teacher thought Moin was doing it, so he was sent to the principal's office. He was waiting outside when Anjali, the head girl, saw him.

'Moin! Where's the piece you promised me for the notice board?'

Moin had completely forgotten about the school notice board. He had told Anjali that he would give her an essay for the wallpaper magazine which they put up on the notice board every week. He had actually wanted to give a drawing, but Anjali looked at his drawings and said, 'They're all too … er … you know, modern? We can't put up abstracts, people won't get it.'

Moin didn't get it, because Moin didn't know what an abstract was. He guessed it was some kind of thing you had to stand on if you couldn't reach high enough while painting the wall.

'But then,' he thought, 'why is Anjali calling my drawing an abstract? You can't stand on it.' He asked Tony, who, of course, knew everything.

'An abstract painting is one where nothing painted bears any resemblance to the world you see with your eyes.'

Moin looked blank.

'Abstract paintings don't have things in them. Or people,' Tony explained.

'But my paintings have things and people and everything. Look there's an apple, and that's a dog and that is a woman watching the dog eat the apple.'

'Oh, is that what it is?' asked Parvati, who had been squinting at the picture from all directions. 'I thought the strange spotted creature was angry because the loaf of bread fell off the table.'

'It's a woman in a polka-dotted sari. And it's an apple, not a loaf of bread,' said Moin, closing the book violently.

He had promised to give Anjali an essay on UFOs instead. But he had not written it.

'Give it to me in the short recess, okay, Moin? We've left a big space for you!' Anjali grinned at Moin and went away.

'This is all your fault,' Moin told the monster. 'If you hadn't made a racket, I wouldn't have been sitting here, and Anjali wouldn't have seen me. Now what am I going to do?'

Before the monster could answer, Moin was called into the principal's office. The

principal's name was. K.K. Kuttykrishnan, but everyone called him Kooki.

'Anh, so what is the problem?' asked Kooki.

'No problem, sir,' Moin said.

'There must be some problem, otherwise you would not be here, no?'

'No, no,' Moin replied, wondering how he should start his essay.

Kooki looked closely at the boy before him. He looked a bit dreamy and he was not smiling or smirking. However, from his experience, he had learnt not to trust innocent-looking schoolboys.

'Are you mocking, enh?'

'No, I'm Moin, sir.'

Kooki thought he might be getting closer to the problem. The child obviously had a problem with English verbs.

'Moing? What is this moing? Did your English teacher send you? You seem to be weak in English. There is no verb like moing.'

'My name is Moin, sir.'

'Did I ask your name, enh?'

Suddenly it dawned on Kooki that he might have been guilty of a great wrong. This boy obviously had a problem understanding the simplest questions. He might be—and at the thought Kooki's little heart swelled with sadness—dyslexic. Or even—his heart swelled a little more—mentally challenged. His eyes softened. His voice softened. His lower lip trembled in sympathy.

'My poor child,' he said. 'My poor, poor child.'

Moin looked around in shock. He had thought he was alone in the room with Kooki. But here was Kooki talking to someone else. He looked everywhere, but could see no one. Then he realised that Kooki was talking to him. He put his head down and tried to force a tear out of his eye by poking a finger into it.

'OW!' yelled Moin. He hadn't expected it to hurt so much.

'Anh, anh, do not cry, son. We all have problems in life. I will talk to your teachers and see that they do not expect too much of you, my poor boy. You may go.'

Moin had no idea why the teachers should not expect too much of him, but it sounded like an excellent idea. 'Thank you s-sir! Y-you are v-very g-g-good sir,' he said, in a trembling voice. He was almost beginning to believe that he was a 'poor boy'.

'Why are you sniffling? Mind you don't drip all over me,' said the monster loudly.

'Who said that?' asked Kooki.

'M-me, sir. Sorry sir,' said Moin and ran out of the room. 'You idiot! You nearly got me into trouble again!' he told his pocket.

In the short recess, Moin began to write the UFO essay. Tony came and took the monster out of Moin's pocket and they chatted about monster rules.

At last, Moin finished his essay with a sigh. Suddenly Parvati appeared at the classroom window.

'Moin! Tony! Come quickly! There's a monkey on the swings.'

The two boys ran to the window.

As they gazed out, Anjali came to the classroom door. She saw Moin at the window.

'Moin! The essay! Quick!'

'It's on my desk, Anjali!' Moin yelled without looking back.

The monster was sitting on Moin's desk, singing squeakily to itself when it saw Anjali coming towards it. It quickly flattened itself and lay quite still.

Anjali saw the essay: 'UFOs: What, How, Why?'

'Nice title,' she thought, and picked it up. Then she caught sight of the monster. 'Oh nice,'

she thought to herself again. 'Moin has done an illustration of an imaginary alien; this will look terrific on the notice board.' She picked it up. The monster was too shocked to make a sound.

'Thanks, Moin!' she shouted as she left.

The bell rang.

The next period was mathematics. Miss Anita came in and peered at Moin. Moin smiled back happily. He liked mathematics, and he liked his mathematics teacher.

Anita frowned. To her eyes, Moin looked perfectly normal. But Kooki had called all the Class IV teachers in the short recess and given them a lecture on how they should be kind to that poor boy Boeing, and not expect too much of him.

It took most of the meeting to figure out who he was talking about.

'Boring?' asked deaf old Mr Gadre. 'My classes are not boring at all. The children love my classes.'

'That's because they don't do anything, Mr G,' snapped Mrs Kapuur, with the two u's. 'But Mr K, sir, there's no Boeing in my class.'

'Small boy, fair, brown eyes, hair falling over his face.'

'Suchitra?' asked Mrs Kapur with one u.

'That's a girl, Mrs K,' said two-u's.

'Good point,' said Mrs Kapur.

Someone thought it might be Tony.

'A Sikh boy, sir?'

'Not exactly sick, but, you know, a little slow. Very sad, enh?'

Finally, Anita hit upon the answer. 'Must be Moin,' she said.

The teachers were all very puzzled, because they thought Moin was a quite a bright boy. A little lazy, but bright. Before they could say anything else, the bell rang.

Now Anita looked carefully to see if there was anything wrong with Moin. 'Are you okay, Moin?' she asked.

'Yes miss!' said Moin.

So Anita carried on with the class. Once in a while she looked at Moin, but he seemed fine.

Moin was beginning to wonder why the

teacher kept looking at him with a frown. He couldn't remember doing anything wrong. Had she seen the monster, he wondered.

He put his hand to his pocket. The monster was not there! Moin felt something jump into his throat. He thought it might be his gall bladder. Or maybe it was his liver. Or even his lungs. Then he remembered that Tony had been talking to the monster in the recess.

He turned to Tony. 'Tony!' he hissed.

Tony looked at Moin, and found him making horrible faces from his desk.

'What?' he whispered.

'Where's the thing?' Moin asked Tony.

'What thing?'

'You know … that …' and he started making horrible faces again. He was trying to look like the monster, but Tony just couldn't understand.

When Moin caught hold of his ears and said, 'Pom! Pom!', Parvati, who sat next to Tony, understood.

Meanwhile, Anita was watching Moin with her mouth open. First, she saw him do strange things with his eyes and nose, and then she clearly saw him hold his ears and heard him go 'Pom! Pom!' Her eyes filled with tears of pity. The boy had obviously had some big shock which had affected his brains. No wonder Kooki had warned the teachers to be good to him. Anita decided she would be very good to Moin.

'Moin, child, what is it?'

Moin jumped up in shock. He hadn't realised that Miss Anita had been watching him.

'N-nothing, miss,' he said.

'Why don't you go to the nurse and ask her to give you some hot chocolate?'

The whole class gasped. The school nurse's hot chocolate was the most delicious thing in the world. All the children wished they would catch a cold during school hours so that they could get the famous hotchoc. They looked enviously at Moin.

Moin went off happily to the school dispensary.

The dispensary was next to the office. Outside the office was the notice board. There was a crowd of people near the board. They were all looking at something and laughing.

Anjali was part of the crowd. She saw Moin and said, 'There he is! Moin, this is fantastic! Great work.'

The crowd moved aside, and Moin saw his essay on the notice board. Also on the board, next to the essay, was the monster.

'Aiy, this thing is awesome. What's it called?' asked Kamal, tapping the monster with his ruler.

'OW!' yelled the monster.

The crowd jumped.

'OW!' yelled Moin quickly. 'Sudden stomach

ache. I always yell OW when that happens. But listen, Anjali, can I take this thing off? I … um … need to make some changes.'

'No way! It's perfect.'

Anjali and the others left.

Moin went towards the monster. It had unflattened itself and looked very funny stuck to the board.

'About time! You're supposed to protect me.'

'Some new monster rule, I suppose,' said Moin bitterly. He was trying to pull off the cellotape. Luckily for the monster, Anjali had decided to stick it to the board, instead of pinning it.

'MOIIIINNNN!'

Moin jumped. It was Anjali. The monster became flat again.

'Why were you trying to take the picture off? I told you to leave it there. If I find you've taken it off, I'll take you straight to the principal. Understand?'

Anjali went off, wagging her finger at Moin.

'Come on, come on, hurry up! It's very uncomfortable hanging in the air like this. Take me off.'

'Can't,' said Moin.

'What do you mean "can't"?'

'You heard her. She'll take me to the principal.'

'So? Why should I care? Anyway, he'll just say "poor boy" and let you go.'

They were still arguing, when Tony and Parvati came running.

'Oh no!' said Tony.

'What an idiot,' said Parvati. Nobody was sure if she meant Moin or the monster.

Parvati and Tony had come to fetch Moin. Miss Anita was getting worried because he'd been away for so long.

'What about MEEEEEE?' wailed the monster.

'We'll think of something,' said Parvati as she and Tony dragged Moin back to class.

'I have to protect it. Monster rule,' Moin told Tony after the maths class.

'It's not a rule. It's not there in my list,' said Tony.

'So what? You know how it keeps remembering new rules every day. If I don't do it, it'll turn me into a suitcase or some other useless thing that I don't want to be.'

'It can't do that. It's not in the rules.'

'I'm not taking any chances. Anyway, we can't leave it there forever. And if anyone finds out it's a monster, all kinds of things might happen.'

'That's true,' said Parvati. 'I only hope it doesn't start singing or dancing.' She gasped. 'Oh god! Anthem practice!'

They looked at each other in horror. The school annual day was coming up, and all the classes had to practise singing the school anthem just before the lunch break. The monster was bound to hear the singing, and start shrieking along in accompaniment.

'No one will hear it,' Tony said, ever hopeful.

Parvati snorted. Moin groaned.

Then Parvati had a brainwave. 'Cellotape its mouth!' she said.

So after the next period, Moin sneaked into the corridor. Tony and Parvati kept watch, while Moin quickly pasted cellotape over the monster's mouth.

'Gllphmgbghfmnnnn!' said the monster.

'It's only for a little while,' Moin whispered and ran back to class.

A few minutes later, anthem practice began. The monster began to twitch. As the singing got louder and stronger, the monster did a wild dance. The cellotape got looser and looser.

Just as the anthem ended, the cellotape came off, and the monster fell down on the floor. It began to run towards Moin's class.

In the lunch break, when Moin, Tony and Parvati scurried to the notice board, the monster was missing.

KOOKI GOES CUCKOO

'I'm telling you, doctor,' said Principal Kuttykrishnan to Dr Reddy, 'I'm going mad! I am seeing things! I am hearing things!'

Dr Reddy clucked. 'Now, now, why don't you tell me all about it, Mr Kuttykrishnan?'

'It was a pink thing.'

'What was?'

'The thing.'

'What thing?'

'The pink thing, I tell you. What is the problem, enh? I'm saying to you that I saw a pink thing. Is this not clear to you? Enh?'

'Er, yes, yes, yes. Go on. What kind of thing was this, er, pink thing?'

'It was an ugly thing.'

'So you saw an ugly pink thing. That is very interesting. A pink ugly thing. Very good.'

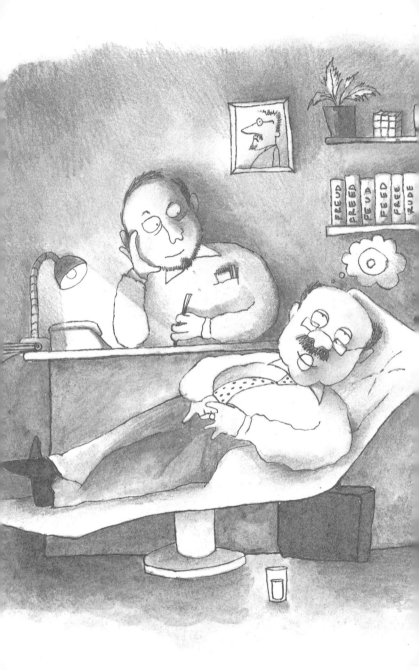

'Good? What is so good about seeing an ugly pink thing when you are eating you're lunch?'

'And where was this thing?'

'In my dustbin.'

'Ah!' Dr Reddy took notes furiously. This had all the signs of being a very interesting case. He could write a paper about it in *Mind Matters*, the most famous psychology journal in the world. 'And why were you looking into your dustbin?' he asked Kooki cunningly.

'Looking into my dustbin? What, do you think I'm mad, enh, to be looking into dustbins?'

As that was exactly what Dr Reddy was beginning to think, he said nothing, but clucked again in a sympathetic sort of way.

'I was having my lunch, when suddenly my dustbin rolled over and fell. Everything fell out, all the trash. I swallowed my vada whole, I was so surprised. Dustbins don't fall by themselves, do they?'

Reddy did not reply. He was busy writing in his book. *Ask for list of items in trash,* he wrote.

'DO THEY?' yelled Kooki.

'What do *you* think?' asked Dr Reddy. 'Do you think they can fall by themselves?'

'I'm asking you,' said Kooki sternly.

'I would say no,' Reddy answered cautiously.

'Anh, exactly. Dustbins do not fall by themselves, I said to myself. So I got up to look, thinking that some cat or rat might have got in.'

Displays logical thinking, wrote Reddy.

'But nothing was there. Simply some paper and some old refills. The usual trash. So I left it like that and went back to eat. Good meal it was. Some good, hot medu-vadas, and sambar. Very good. That Sriram Bhavan food is quite tasty, enh? They send me a tiffin every day.' Kooki drooled for a moment.

Reddy wrote, *Obsessed with food?*

'So then I started singing.'

'Haanh?' asked Reddy, startled out of his polished manner. But he quickly recovered. 'That's very interesting,' he said. 'Do you often indulge in, er, vocal music?'

'When I have had a good meal, and my stomach is full, I feel very satisfied. And when I am in a good, happy mood, I sing. I am told my voice is not bad. Not bad at all. Do you want me to sing?'

'The question is, do you want to sing?' asked Dr Reddy.

'I have not eaten. But I should explain what happened, so I will sing. You will get a clear picture then. I started singing the school anthem.'

We are the students of MPKC school
Scholarship and leadership is our cherished goal
Whether it is studies or whether it's a game
To MPKC school we will bring pride and fame.

Dr Reddy winced. Mr Kuttykrishnan beamed.

'Nice, enh? My tune. The words are not exactly mine. Our English teacher did the lyrics. I wanted to say "pride and name" but she wanted "fame". So I said, name, fame, same thing.'

'Very interesting,' Dr Reddy said faintly. His ears were still ringing from Kooki's bellowing.

Suddenly Kooki scowled. 'But as I was singing, suddenly one horrible voice started singing with me. It was changing all the words. It sang something like this—'

In a high-pitched voice, Kooki began to sing:

We are the students of MPKC school
When we see bananas we begin to drool
Whether it is studies or whether it's a game
We don't really care because to us it's all the same.

Dr Reddy searched desperately for cotton to stuff in his ears. One more song like that and he would go deaf.

'And that,' said Kooki, 'was when I saw it. The ugly pink thing. It was standing on the pile of trash, doctor, and *singing*!'

Hallucinations, wrote Dr Reddy. His ears still felt tender, but he did not want to miss anything. 'Did you talk to this, er, thing?' he asked.

'I was just about to, when the door shot open and three students rushed into the room. I was very relieved to see them. That ugly pink thing might have attacked me if I was alone. Come to think of it, I don't know why they did not knock. Very uncouth. But at that time, I forgot to ask them all that. I pointed at the pink thing.

'"What is that?" I asked.

'But you know what they said, doctor?'

'Why don't *you* tell me?' Dr Reddy asked gently. This was getting very exciting, and his pen flew over his paper.

'They said there was nothing there. I asked them if they had heard the horrible singing, and they said that they had never heard so much silence in their lives. I was shocked, I tell you. Either they were lying, or I was having— what do you call them?—hallucinations, yes. So I went to the dustbin. Slowly. When I reached there, what did I find? That pink thing, that ugly thing, was actually just a drawing on paper!

'"This thing was singing!" I told the children.

'"This, sir?" said that boy whose name I forget. Aeroplane, I think. Or maybe it is Jumbo

Jet. Anyway, he said, "This is my drawing of an alien, sir. It fell off the notice board. I was looking for it."

'Then I remembered, I had picked up a piece of paper just outside my room, and put it in the dustbin. So it *was* a drawing. As soon as the children left, I locked up my office and rushed here.'

Dr Reddy sighed in satisfaction. There was silence for a moment.

'Am I going mad, doctor?' asked Kooki.

'What do *you* think?' asked Dr Reddy gently.

That evening, Parvati, Tony and Moin sat in Moin's room. The monster was lying on the windowsill and eating dates, which Tony had brought for it.

'What luck we heard it. I thought we were never going to find it,' said Tony.

'Luck? What if Kooki had caught it? I would be done for.'

'When I heard the song coming through Kooki's door, I nearly died of fright. But what I want to know,' said Parvati, 'is, how did the monster get there?'

They turned to the monster. It was trying to crack a date seed with its blunt teeth. When

it saw they were all waiting for an answer, it
began to sing:

Humans, these humans, are foolish, it is plain
They don't know how to use their eyes or ears or nose
or brain
I was running to the classroom
Through the corridor
When suddenly a tiny man
Came out of a door
Flattened, like a paper
I lay down on the floor,

He threw me in the dustbin
Oh, I'm still feeling sore

Humans, these humans, are really foolish creatures
The students are idiotic, but worse still are the teachers.

Parvati stuffed a date in the monster's mouth to stop it singing.

Not a minute too soon. Moin's mother came in with some sandwiches and a bunch of bananas.

Humans, these humans, are ill-mannered and rude
What makes them somewhat bearable is all their yummy food!

—sang the monster, swallowing the date whole and grabbing the bunch of bananas as soon as she left the room.

Outside the door, Mrs Kaif shook her head. 'Those singing lessons aren't doing Moin any good,' she thought sadly.

HAIR CARE

'I've just remembered a rule: I can change the way I look within reasonable limits,' the monster told Moin.

MONSTER RULE 47

A monster can alter its appearance within reasonable limits.

'What does that mean? Reasonable limits?' asked Moin.

'It means I can't change these stupid honking ears or these drumstick legs or these brooms you've given me instead of feet.'

'It's not my fault, your descriptions were all wrong.'

The monster ignored Moin. 'But I can do something about this frizzy hair. Look, I want hair like this.'

The monster was looking at the pictures in a film magazine, which Moin had found in the old suitcase under his bed. The magazine had photographs of all the famous film stars with their coiffed, beauty-salon hair. The monster was pointing at the picture of a particularly well-known actress.

'That's a woman,' said Moin. Suddenly, a thought struck him. 'Are you a girl?'

'We don't have these silly human distinctions.'

MONSTER RULE 4

A monster is neither masculine nor feminine.

'It's not silly.'

'It is to monsters. And anyway, it's very silly if it means you can't have the kind of hair you like, or wear the clothes you want to wear or do the things you want to do. If I want hair like this, I can have hair like this.'

'No, you can't. She has such silky, soft hair. Yours will never be like that.'

'I'll ask Tony how to do it. He'll know, he has long hair.'

'Maybe you should tie up your hair the way Tony does.' He tied up the monster's hair in a knot on top of its head, and bundled the knot up in a handkerchief. 'How's that?' he asked.

'It doesn't suit my personality. I should have long hair, because I have an artistic personality. I have music in my soul. Long, flowing hair goes well with music in the soul.'

'I wish it would stay in your soul, instead of coming out of your mouth,' Moin muttered.

But Moin's wish did not come true. In a nasal, soulful way, the monster started to sing:

Hair hair, cowlick and care
Freshly fine and frizzy
Fair fair, blithe as a bear
Grizzly bees are busy

Tan tan, oil in the pan
Smooth red wine and sipping
Man man, head in a can
Seventy-nine and dipping.

'Imagine how much better it would be if I had hair falling on my cheek while I sang that.'

'Imagine how much better it would be if you didn't sing at all.'

'The problem,' said the monster to Moin, 'is that you have no music in your soul.'

It spent the rest of the morning driving Moin crazy singing mournful songs sung in its high-pitched, shrieky voice and sweeping around the room with its broom-feet.

Outside, Mr and Mrs Kaif were having a serious discussion.

'Moin seems to be really keen on his singing. He's been practising all day,' said Mrs Kaif.

There was silence. Neither of them wanted to admit what they really felt about their son's musical abilities.

Finally, Mr Kaif said: 'At any rate, Chowdhuryji seems to think he's very good. I met him at the fish market one day, and he told me he wants Moin to do a public performance.'

There was another miserable silence. Mrs Kaif had a sudden blinding image of her family and friends at Moin's concert making a dash for the doors the moment Moin started singing. Mr Kaif hoped Chowdhuryji would inform them in time, so he could plan a business trip on the day of the performance.

'Can one go senile at sixty?' Mrs Kaif asked her husband. She could think of no other explanation for Chowdhuryji's strange desire to unleash Moin's singing on the world at large.

'It's …' began Mr Kaif, and stopped, because Moin came dashing into the room. He was on his way to his parents' bathroom to get some hair oil and shampoo for the monster.

He stopped when he saw his parents. They looked guilty for some reason.

'Moin, come and sit here.'

Moin sat, but he was very nervous. The monster was in a singing mood today. He had told it not to make a sound till he got back, he had even managed to shut it up by giving it some sticky toffee to eat. But he wasn't sure how long the effect of the toffee or the order to keep quiet would last.

'Do you like Chowdhuryji?' Moin's father began, delicately.

'Yup,' replied Moin.

'Do you find him, you know, *odd,* in any way?'

Moin thought. 'He has strange hair,' he said finally. He had hair on his mind.

'No, apart from the hair. Does he say strange things, for example? Does he do anything, um, strange?'

Moin tried to remember. 'He dug his nose once, and wiped his hand on the cushion,' he said at last. 'But he had a bad cold,' he added quickly, because he liked his singing teacher.

'That's not strange, it's just bad upbringing,' said Mrs Kaif looking pointedly at Mr Kaif.

'I don't do it anymore,' Mr Kaif mumbled.

Moin thought harder. 'He sings very loudly. Can I go now?' He got up and headed for the bathroom door.

'Maybe he's deaf!' Mrs Kaif exclaimed happily.

'Where are you going?' Mr Kaif asked Moin.

'I want some hair oil and shampoo and conditioner. My hair's getting really rough.'

Mr and Mrs Kaif looked at each other in alarm. Since Moin had sleek hair that flopped over his forehead, they could only conclude that he was becoming very vain.

Over the past few weeks, Mr and Mrs Kaif had been getting concerned about Moin. He had changed a lot. He had started eating too much, for one thing. He could polish off a dozen bananas at once. He had developed a sudden craving for dates and toffees and needed to have some in his room all the time. Oddly enough, it didn't seem to have any effect on his weight.

He was also getting very particular about his privacy. He didn't like anyone entering his room without knocking. Usually Mrs Kaif would have to clean out his room thoroughly every few weeks, but now, it was not only tidy, but always swept and clean so that she never needed to go in at all. And to make doubly sure that no one entered his room, Moin kept it locked when he went out.

Then, of course, there was the singing. If he sang nice songs, they might not have minded so much. Some song from a Hindi film for instance, or even the classical songs that he was learning from Chowdhuryji. But he seemed to be inventing his own songs, with meaningless words and horrible tunes. His voice, they felt, he could not help. He used to have a sweet enough voice when he was small, but around the time that he started eating a lot, even his voice seemed to have changed.

They were still looking at each other in perplexity, when Moin dashed out of the bathroom.

'Thanks!' he yelled as he ran to his room.

Soon, the singing began again. Moin's parents sat together in sorrowful silence. Though they were good parents, who believed in letting their child be whoever he wanted to be, they couldn't help wishing he would be a normal kind of child, unwashed and untidy and careless. They just could not understand this new, neat boy, whose teachers called to tell them that they should handle him with sensitivity.

And now he was even conditioning his hair.

'Maybe he's just growing up,' Mr Kaif said hopefully.

Back in his own bathroom, Moin put a chair near the wash basin, and a couple of pillows on the chair. The monster stood on them, with its head bent over the basin.

MONSTER RULE 321

Human products can have unpredictable side-effects on monsters.

Moin poured water on the monster's head, and began to rub shampoo on its hair.

Suddenly, a very scary thing happened. Moin could feel the hair beginning to move. When he looked down at the monster's head, he saw that its hair was growing and growing.

'Your hair's getting longer!' he cried.

'Ogulb,' said the monster. It had got some water in its nose. It was quite pleased at Moin's announcement, because Kapeera Kanoor, the glamorous actress in the magazine, had very long hair.

Moin, on the other hand, was not pleased at all. Before his horrified eyes the monster's hair grew, past its shoulders, down to its waist.

'It must be the shampoo!' he realised suddenly. He grabbed a bucket of water and poured it over the monster's head.

The monster fell headlong into the basin. As the water spiralled through the drainage hole, the monster started screeching and thrashing about. By the time the water had gone, its hair had got into a horrible tangle. Moin lifted the monster out.

'Why couldn't you let it grow?' asked the monster.

'I had to stop it some time! It's quite long now.'

But since the monster's hair was bunched up in a tangled knot it was difficult to convince it that its hair had grown down to its knees. Moin had no idea how to get rid of the knots. Finally, they called Tony.

Tony came and stared at the monster for a long time.

'Did you try oil?' he asked finally.

'No. What if something else happens because of the oil?'

'Can't you think of any hair rules?' Tony asked the monster.

'No,' said the monster, scowling.

'Once, my cousin got chewing gum in his hair and they had to cut it off,' Tony said.

'I'm not letting you cut my hair.'

'And once, another cousin washed his hair with soap. I think it was Squiril soap. He was very sleepy so he didn't rinse it off properly, and he went to sleep while his hair was still damp. When he woke up all his hair had fallen off.'

Moin and the monster looked at Tony expectantly. Tony looked back solemnly.

Finally, Moin said, 'Then?'

'What do you mean "then"?'

'What was the point of that story? How does it help us?'

'Oh, it doesn't. I just thought it might amuse you.'

'We are not amused,' the monster said, sulkily, looking longingly at the photograph of Kappera Kanoor's lovely hair.

'What do you do when your hair gets all knotted up?'

'My mother oils it for me, and then disentangles the knots.'

'Do you think we should try the oil then?'

'Hmm. Maybe we should try it on a small patch first. Minimize the effects.'

'Okay, so if anything happens, it'll happen only in a small bit.'

They sat the monster on a chair and Tony, since he was acknowledged to be the expert, started oiling a part of the monster's hair. They waited to see if anything would happen. Nothing did.

So Tony started taking out the knots.

'More oil,' he said.

Moin poured some more oil out of the bottle on to the monster's head. Tony smeared it in the monster's hair and started to unknot it.

'No side-effects, thankfully,' said Moin, speaking too soon, as usual.

Because the moment he said this, he noticed that the monster's head was looking rather big. Sure enough, as the oil began to soak into the monster's head, the head started to grow.

The choice was between a big head and long hair. To wash off the oil they would have to use shampoo, and that would make the monster's hair grow. But if they did not get rid of the oil at once, they had no idea how big the head would grow. For all they knew, it might never stop growing.

'At least the hair can be cut!' shouted Moin, rushing to the bathroom with the monster.

Tony went to help him. They washed and rinsed and when they were done the monster's hair was so long that it trailed behind it as it walked.

It was very pleased, of course. It paraded around the room, crooning (if a shrieky-moany kind of sound can be called crooning):

Hair so long
Hai-ir so lo-ong
Makes me want to
Break into so-ong

Song so sweet
So-ong so swe-eet

Makes me want
To tap my fe-eet.

The monster tried to do a little dance as it
sang this, but it tripped on its hair and fell
over. Tony and Moin rolled on the floor
laughing.

The monster was offended. 'It's not funny.
What am I to do?'

'I'll cut it for you,' Tony offered.

'Oh, oh. I've just remembered a monster
rule about hair.'

'Just remembered?' asked Moin. 'You mean
you just made it up.'

'No I didn't. We can't make up rules. I told
you, there's a rule about that.'

'Wait! Let me write this down.' Tony took out the *Monster Rule Book* he was writing.

MONSTER RULE 93

A monster cannot get rid of any bodily part it acquires in the human world.

'A hair is a bodily part isn't it? So there, I can't have my hair cut.'

'It depends on what they mean by body,' said Moin. 'If they mean body as separate from head—you know, like head and body – then the hair is part of the head, not the body, and you can cut it.'

'Why don't we try? We'll see what happens.' In addition to his *Rule Book*, Tony was also writing a book called *The Strange Behaviour of Monsters*. He had found that though the monster was quite happy to tell him all the monster rules that it could remember, it never told him anything else about the monster world. So he had to get his information on monster behaviour from observing the monster. He was eager to see what happened if a rule was broken.

The monster reluctantly agreed to cut its hair. It liked its hair, but it wanted to be able to dance. So it sat on a chair and Moin brought out his scissors.

But Moin could not cut the monster's hair. It was very strange. The scissors snipped through the hair, but the hair stayed uncut. Moin kept trying, then Tony gave it a go, but the hair just would not get cut.

So finally Tony and Moin made two plaits of the monster's hair, and coiled them round into two buns on either side of its head.

'Now you look like an alien.' Suddenly Tony went tomato-red with excitement. 'Alien!' he croaked. 'Why didn't I think of it before! Maybe it's not a monster at all, but an alien! An extra-terrestrial.'

'You think so?' asked Moin. 'It says it's a monster, and it was under my bed, remember?'

'But that's the whole point. We don't know what aliens are like. Maybe they are monsters, who knows? We should have thought of it before; remember even our head girl Anjali mistook it for an alien. We should find out where it's come from!'

'And where it can go back to,' Moin said.

'Are you an alien, is that what you are? An extra-terrestrial from outer space?' Tony asked the monster.

'I wish you wouldn't use all these big words,' said the monster. 'They make me sleepy.' It curled up on the sheets in the cupboard and fell asleep.

'You know, I've always believed that there was intelligent life in outer space,' said Tony.

Moin looked at the monster with its two buns sticking out like ears, and its mouth open as it slept in the cupboard. 'Intelligent' was not the word that came to his mind, but if it meant he could get rid of the monster, he was ready to believe anything.

MONSTER TAKES A RIDE

MONSTER RULE 54

A monster has to stay for ever with the human who has given it a body. (Also see rules number 71, 228 and 364.)

'I knew it! I knew there was a peephole,' Moin cried in excitement.

'A peephole?' asked Parvati.

'You know, when there's a way out of a rule. I'm sure there's a peephole in Rules 71, 228 and 364. Some except-if , you know. Like—a monster has to stay forever with the human who has given it a body, except if.'

'He means a loophole,' Tony explained to Parvati, who was frowning very hard. 'But the monster can't remember 71, 228 or 364. It says it might have even got the numbers wrong. The only thing to do is to find out which planet it is from.'

Tony was still convinced that the monster was an alien from outer space, though all his attempts to talk to the monster about it had failed. The moment he mentioned galaxies the monster would start yawning, and when he got to the business of interplanetary communication, all he got in reply was a snore. In fact, the monster was fast asleep, while Tony, Moin and Parvati discussed it.

'My uncle Harimama has a telescope,' said Parvati.

'So? My Jaspaluncle has a microscope,' said Tony.

'So? My Sameeruncle has a stethoscope,' said Moin.

'You're so stupid, it's not a competition. We can show the monster the planets through

Harimama's telescope, and see if it recognises its home.'

Moin and Tony were speechless with admiration for a minute or two.

'But will he allow us?'

'We can't give him the real reason.'

'He's always going on about how young children should take an interest in astronomy. We'll tell him we've started a Star-gazing Club. He'll be very pleased.'

So a couple of nights later, on the weekend, Parvati, Tony and Moin went to spend the night at Harimama's house. To make it look official, Moin had made badges for all of them.

Parvati refused to wear the badge at first.

'What are these squiggles on the badge? They look icky—like tadpoles.'

'They're stars. You're blind.'

'But stars don't have tails.'

'They're shooting stars, stupid. These are normal stars.' Moin pointed at a couple of things that looked like flowers with strangely-shaped petals.

Finally, Parvati gave in, because Moin had written 'Star-gazing Club' in beautiful handwriting and the badge looked quite nice if you ignored all the stars.

So they all trooped into Parvati's uncle's

house wearing their badges. As soon as they entered they saw a huge dog.

The dog bounded up to Parvati and licked her till she was dripping wet and smelly. Then he sniffed at Tony and licked his face in greeting. But when he came to Moin, he began to growl.

'Nice doggie, nice doggie,' Moin squeaked, hoping the massive creature wouldn't eat him up. He looked hungry.

'Hey, Small, what's up? Friends! Friends!' Harimama called.

'Small?' asked Tony and Moin.

'Ah, just my little joke. Ha! Ha!' Harimama was a large man, and when he laughed the windows rattled and flakes of paint came loose and floated down gently from the ceiling.

Meanwhile, Small, looking decidedly big and menacing to Moin's terrified eyes, was circling round and round Moin.

'Why me?' asked Moin, when suddenly the answer came to him through a shiver in his pocket. The monster was hiding in Moin's shirt pocket as usual, and Small had smelt it out.

Moin looked at Parvati and Tony, who, instead of understanding the seriousness of the situation, grinned idiotically at him. He tried to point at his pocket with his eyes.

'Does your friend have a squint?' Harimama whispered to his niece.

'No, I don't …' she began, and gasped as she saw Moin's pocket give a sudden jump.

'What is it?'

'Harimama! Moin is allergic to dogs! He's getting the Doggy Squint. He always gets it when he's around dogs. You'll have to shut Small up.'

'Now, now, Parvati, you know I never shut him up. Against my principles. Why don't we shut your friend up, then, eh? Would that be alright? Eh Moin?' Moin looked petrified.

'Just joking! Ha, ha! Ha, ha, ha!' Some more paint gently snowed down in flakes from the ceiling. 'He'll get used to you. Don't worry. He's just getting used to your smell. Had a bath today, I hope? Ha, ha!'

Small, meanwhile, had zeroed in on Moin's pocket. Moin froze while the dog sniffed wetly at the monster.

To distract her uncle, Parvati started talking to him about coconut oil, which was the first thing that came to her mind.

This was lucky, because the monster suddenly decided to un-flatten itself. It hopped out of Moin's pocket, and on to Small's back.

Small got the fright of his life. The front door was open, and Small shot out of it, whining and yelping at the top of his voice.

'Oh no!' Moin shouted and ran after the dog.

'Get him!' Tony shouted and ran after Moin.

'Don't worry, he'll be back!' yelled Harimama.

'Whoosh!' yelled Parvati, determined to prevent Harimama from running after them.

Harimama looked at her in shock.

'Whoosh. That's the noise that coconut trees make when the wind blows through them.' From coconut oil to coconut trees seemed like a logical move to Parvati, but it seemed to have taken her uncle completely by surprise.

'Coconut trees?' he asked. When he had agreed to have the children over he had imagined a nice, peaceful night, looking at the stars, and creating in young minds a lifelong fascination for astronomy. Things didn't seem to be moving in that direction. One young mind seemed to be obsessed with, of all things, coconuts, while neither of the other two children had shown any signs of a mind at all.

Outside, the dog was running round and round in circles. Fortunately he seemed to have a territory. He ran up to the end of the road, then did a sharp turn, almost a U, then he ran till he reached a red postbox and turned left into a lane which curved in a crescent and joined the main road again. In this area marked by the end of the road, the postbox and the crescent-shaped lane, the dog ran around, chased by Moin and Tony who were singing at the top of their voices to the disgust or amusement of the passers-by, depending on their disposition.

The reason for their sudden musical fit was not far to seek, if anyone tried to seek it, which, luckily, they did not. The monster, after the first shock of movement was enjoying itself immensely. It was singing a happy ditty in rhythm with the galloping of the poor, confused dog:

Ho ho! Go go go
Go dog go
Go fast not slow.

What what! Trot trot trot
Trot dog trot
Though horse you're not.

Son son! Run run run
Run dog run
Oh run for fun!

Moin and Tony were trying to drown out its voice.

At some point, Small decided that enough was enough. Whether he was tired, or whether the monster's horrible singing just got too much for him is anybody's guess. He skidded to a stop.

The monster was taken by surprise. It whizzed over Small's head and landed in some bushes on the side of the road.

Tony ran and grabbed hold of Small's collar, while Moin searched for the monster in the bushes. It was nowhere to be found.

It was early evening and it was beginning to get dark.

'What should we do?' hissed Moin, when he saw Harimama come towards them, with Parvati pulling at his kurta behind him, and trying to tell him a story about a boy who climbed up a coconut tree.

'What's up, there? What are you doing in the bushes, Moin?'

'I lost my-my …'

'Gold ring!' shouted Parvati. 'Your ring, Moin! Where is it?'

'Ring? What …'

'The ring! Which fell into the bushes!' Parvati said, blinking so hard that her eyelashes nearly fell off. She was actually trying to wink, but she could never manage to close one eye without closing the other.

'Ah yes! My ring! It fell in the bushes, that's right.'

'You'll need a torch,' said Harimama. He took Small and went off into the house.

'Quick,' said Tony, 'Let's sing a song. That's the only way to locate it.'

Tony, Moin and Parvati stood around the bushes and sang the national anthem, much to the amazement of the neighbours and passers-by. Some of them even stopped and stood at attention.

There was not a squeak in reply.

They all went into the bushes to look for the monster, though it was too dark to see anything.

Moin began to get very worried. 'What if it was bitten by a snake? What if it was eaten by a rat? What if it hit its head and died of head injury? What if …'

Praap!

Moin jumped about three and a half feet into the air.

'What was that?' asked Parvati and Tony, as they came running towards Moin.

'It sounded like a—'

'Like an autorickshaw horn!' said a familiar shrieky-gruff voice, sounding very grumpy. 'You stepped on my ear. Monster ears should be sharp and scary, but no! You have to give me ears that go praap! when you press them.'

'What were you doing there on the ground?' asked Moin.

'Trying to get some sleep, of course,' said the monster bitterly. 'It's very tiring to ride a dog. But you blew my horn and woke me up.'

'Sleep? Here? Have you any idea how worried—' Parvati began.

'Quick!' Tony said. 'Harimama!'

Moin quickly stuffed the monster into his pocket.

'Here's the torch,' said Harimama.

Harimama shone the torch into the bushes and they all searched for the nonexistent ring.

Moin, to create some excitement, suddenly shouted, 'There!'

And when Harimama shone the torch at the point where he was pointing, he sighed dramatically and said, 'Oh, it's just some paper.'

Once, Parvati yelled, 'Aha!' But when they all turned round to look, they found that she had only managed to kill a mosquito that had landed on her arm.

Finally, Moin said sadly, 'Never mind, uncle, it's just a ring. I'll tell my mother I lost it.'

'Come, come, we'll go and look at the stars,' said Harimama, patting Moin kindly on the head. 'Then you'll feel much better.'

FOREVER, MOIN

'You and your bright ideas,' Moin told Parvati the next day. They were all at Moin's house.

'It's not my fault if your brainless monster stuck its head into the telescope and couldn't come out. Now Harimama will never let me use his telescope again.'

'I've never seen a grown man cry,' said Tony in a voice full of awe.

'Don't you dare tell anyone!' shouted Parvati. 'He loves his telescope, so how do you think he felt when he saw it broken? It's all your fault, with your stupid ideas of aliens and intelligent creatures from outer space. Anyone with half an eye can see that the monster is the most unintelligent thing in the world.'

They all looked at the monster. Its mouth was full of bananas and milk. It was trying to shake itself so it could make a banana milkshake.

'What do we do now?' asked Moin.

'I hate to say this, but I think you'll just have to learn to live with it. It's not a bad sort. Just a bit odd.'

'Easy for you to say. You only have to make your list of rules, and see it once in a while.

I have to feed it tons of bananas every day, I have to bear its horrible—'

Shake, shake, banana shake

Make, make, a milky lake

Bake, bake, a duck and a drake

Fake, fake, for goodness' sake

Snake, snake, a slimy cake

Take, take, arise and—

'Bye Moin!' yelled Tony and ran.

'Er, have to go now,' said Parvati and left.

Awaaaake!!!

'Nice friends,' Moin said bitterly. 'Leaving me alone with this cacophony.'

'Cacophony? I like that! When I was just trying to cheer you up because you were all looking glum. It goes against my nature to sing such frivolous songs. I have a deep sort of soul, I only like to sing deep sort of songs.'

It began to sing in a soulful voice:

Nobody cares to hear me sing
Everybody thinks I'm bad
Nobody wants to hear my voice
Oh it makes me sad.

I have to stay in this house for good
It's here that I belong
But oh it's hard to stay in a place
Where nobody wants my song.

Mr and Mrs Kaif, busy writing out invitations to Moin's singing concert which Chowdhuryji had fixed for the following week, stopped to listen.

'Poor boy,' said Mrs Kaif, with tears in her eyes. 'We really must be more encouraging.'

'Yes,' agreed Mr Kaif, bravely deciding not to leave town before the concert.

In Moin's room, the monster was standing on the windowsill in a tragic pose and singing.

'Get off! Someone will see you!' said Moin.

The monster ignored him.

Nobody wants to see my face
Oh it makes me cry
Nobody wants to have me here
I really don't know why ...

'Stop it!' yelled Moin.

'But it's true. You don't want me to stay. You're trying to send me off to some other planet or something. I'm a monster, not some strange unearthly creature.'

And it started singing again:

Nobody thinks I ought to stay
They think that I should go
They say that I'm an alien
And make me feel so low.

'Alright, alright,' said Moin. 'You're not an alien.'

'And you won't try to send me away?'
'No.'
'And you'll feed me well?'
'Yes.'
'Bananas?'
'Yes.'
'And dates?'
'Yes.'
'And you'll take me to school sometimes?'
'Yes.'

'And you'll listen to my songs?'

'Er, yes!'

'I don't believe you.'

'I will.'

'Say it.'

'I will listen,' said Moin through gritted teeth.

'Properly.'

'I WILL LISTEN TO YOUR SONGS!'

'Promise?'

'PROMISE!'

The monster grinned and jumped off the windowsill.

'Okay, then I don't mind staying here forever.'

'Oh joy,' said Moin.

Turn the page for a sneak peek ...

'You haven't told me any new rules in a long time,' Tony complained to the monster.

Tony was trying to write two books at the same time. He had started off with *The Monster Rule Book*. But now he was also writing *The Strange Behaviour of Monsters*. Since the monster always behaved strangely, this book was much thicker than the rule book.

The monster couldn't remember all the rules. Whenever it remembered one suddenly, Tony wrote it down. The monster also remembered them in random order, so Tony had more gaps than rules.

'Ha. Rules, my left toe,' Moin muttered. He was convinced the monster was making up the rules.

'I told you there's a rule about making rules,' the monster said.

'It's true,' said Tony. 'See rule number 18.'

'Ha. Number eighteen, my purple toenail,' muttered Moin.

'Hey! I want to paint my toenails purple!'

'You don't have toenails,' Moin pointed out.

'And whose fault is that?' asked the monster. 'Did I ask you to make my feet look like brooms? Now the least you can do is help these ugly broom-feet look pretty. I can paint the edges purple.'

'Purple! Such an ugly colour!' said Moin.

The monster stood on top of Moin's bed and scowled. 'Purple is the best colour in the world! I was supposed to be purple, and you made me pink. Just because you didn't have a purple crayon,' it added bitterly. 'I would have looked magnificent in purple. Now I look like a … like a … baby's bottom!'

'My baby cousin's bottom is not pink, it's brown,' said Moin.

The monster sighed. 'You're missing the point. As usual.' He turned to Tony. 'You tell me. Wouldn't I have totally rocked in deep purple?'

'You look very nice in pink,' said Tony, who thought the monster was the best thing that had ever happened. He was glad it had chosen Moin's bed to hide under, though. Tony didn't think he could have dealt with its singing and its appetite for bananas.

But the monster was looking really sad about being pink.

'Maybe we can change your colour,' said Tony, feeling sorry for it. 'Is there a monster rule that says you can't? If you could grow your hair, you could change your colour, surely. They're both enhancements.'

The monster yawned.

'Big word,' it said.

'Oh,' said Tony. He had forgotten that big words made the monster sleepy. 'What I mean,' he explained, 'is that Monster Rule 47 says that "a monster can alter its appearance within reasonable limits." That means you can change how you look up to a point. So maybe you can change your colour to purple.'

Anushka Ravishankar is a children's writer based in Delhi. She has written over twenty books for children, many of which have received international awards. Her books include the *Zain and Ana* series, *Elephants Never Forget*, *Song of the Bookworm* and *To Market! To Market!* Several of her books have been translated into Dutch, German, Italian, Spanish and other languages.

Anitha Balachandran makes a precarious living as a award-winning animation film-maker and illustrator. Her work has been exhibited and published internationally. Her present preoccupations include stories about animals, stories for and about children and of old people. You might pass her in the street if you happen to be in Delhi.